THE
COW-TAIL SWITCH

THE
COW-TAIL SWITCH

AND OTHER WEST AFRICAN STORIES

by HAROLD COURLANDER *and* GEORGE HERZOG

DRAWINGS BY MADYE LEE CHASTAIN

HOLT, RINEHART AND WINSTON
NEW YORK · CHICAGO · SAN FRANCISCO

CONTENTS

THE
COW-TAIL SWITCH

"AFRICA IS MANY THINGS"

AFRICA is many things. It is a continent of great rivers and deep forests, of deserts and mountains. In the north there are great stretches of sand where nothing grows, where the days are insufferably hot and the nights bitter cold. Near the equator, from Cameroon through the vast Congo River country, are dense rain forests, and in the east, in Kenya, are towering mountain peaks which are white with snow all the year around.

The peoples of Africa are many things, too. They speak many different languages, so that those on the Gulf of Guinea don't understand the speech of those who live in the Nile Valley, and the Kaffirs of the south don't understand the people of the north. Even in that part of West Africa bulging into the Atlantic, the people of one tribe may not understand the speech of their nearest neighbors.

Many Africans have their villages near the jungles and forests, others live on the seacoast, in the hills, along the rivers, or in the grasslands. Some wrest their livelihood from nature by fishing in the sea or in inland lakes, some by farming or cattle-raising, some by hunting, some by trading. There are country people and townspeople, tiny villages and great cities, and among them are iron workers, bronze and brass casters, wood carvers, and shopkeepers.

In the westward bulge of Africa, from Cameroon to Senegal, there were once great kingdoms. There have been wars among some of them, and tribal migrations. Europeans have come and colonized. In the big cities along the coast the old way of life has changed a little, but many old things have not changed, like their music, dancing, and telling of stories.

Generation after generation of West Africans have

told their stories among themselves. Whenever people moved from one place to another they took their stories with them. When they came to the New World as slaves they brought their stories along, and you may hear some of them today as Br'er Rabbit tales in the United States or as Bouqui and Anancy tales in the West Indies and South America.

The stories of West Africa are about men and animals, about kings, warriors, and hunters. They tell about clever people and stupid people, about good ones and bad ones, about how things and animals got to be how they are. Sometimes they are just tall tales. There are stories about Frog, Rabbit, Turtle, Guinea Fowl, and all the other animals that West Africans know. Some of the stories make you think. Some make you laugh.

Here are some of the stories of the people of the forests, the seacoast, the hills, and the plains.

The people of West Africa give them to you.

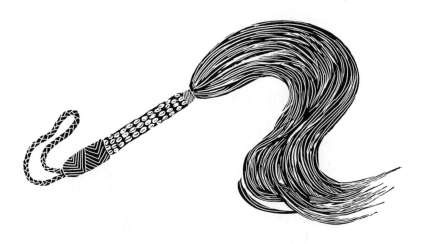

THE
COW=TAIL SWITCH

NEAR the edge of the Liberian rain forest, on a hill overlooking the Cavally River, was the village of Kundi. Its rice and cassava fields spread in all directions. Cattle grazed in the grassland near the river. Smoke from the fires in the round clay houses seeped through the palmleaf roofs, and from a distance these faint columns of smoke seemed to hover over the village. Men and boys fished in the river with nets, and women pounded grain in wooden mortars before the houses.

In this village, with his wife and many children, lived a hunter by the name of Ogaloussa.

5

One morning Ogaloussa took his weapons down from the wall of his house and went into the forest to hunt. His wife and his children went to tend their fields, and drove their cattle out to graze. The day passed, and they ate their evening meal of manioc and fish. Darkness came, but Ogaloussa didn't return.

Another day went by, and still Ogaloussa didn't come back. They talked about it and wondered what could have detained him. A week passed, then a month. Sometimes Ogaloussa's sons mentioned that he hadn't come home. The family cared for the crops, and the sons hunted for game, but after a while they no longer talked about Ogaloussa's disappearance.

Then, one day, another son was born to Ogaloussa's wife. His name was Puli. Puli grew older. He began to sit up and crawl. The time came when Puli began to talk, and the first thing he said was, "Where is my father?"

The other sons looked across the ricefields.

"Yes," one of them said. "Where is Father?"

"He should have returned long ago," another one said.

"Something must have happened. We ought to look for him," a third son said.

"He went into the forest, but where will we find him?" another one asked.

"I saw him go," one of them said. "He went that way, across the river. Let us follow the trail and search for him."

So the sons took their weapons and started out to look for Ogaloussa. When they were deep among the great trees and vines of the forest they lost the trail. They searched in the forest until one of them found the trail again. They followed it until they lost the way once more, and then another son found the trail. It was dark in the forest, and many times they became lost. Each time another son found the way. At last they came to a clearing among the trees, and there on the ground scattered about lay Ogaloussa's bones and his rusted weapons. They knew then that Ogaloussa had been killed in the hunt.

One of the sons stepped forward and said, "I know how to put a dead person's bones together." He gathered all of Ogaloussa's bones and put them together, each in its right place.

7

Another son said, "I have knowledge too. I know how to cover the skeleton with sinews and flesh." He went to work, and he covered Ogaloussa's bones with sinews and flesh.

A third son said, "I have the power to put blood into a body." He went forward and put blood into Ogaloussa's veins, and then he stepped aside.

Another of the sons said, "I can put breath into a body." He did his work, and when he was through they saw Ogaloussa's chest rise and fall.

"I can give the power of movement to a body," another of them said. He put the power of movement into his father's body, and Ogaloussa sat up and opened his eyes.

"I can give him the power of speech," another son said. He gave the body the power of speech, and then he stepped back.

Ogaloussa looked around him. He stood up.

"Where are my weapons?" he asked.

They picked up his rusted weapons from the grass where they lay and gave them to him. They then returned the way they had come, through the forest and the ricefields, until they had arrived once more in the village.

Ogaloussa went into his house. His wife prepared a bath for him and he bathed. She prepared food for

8

him and he ate. Four days he remained in the house, and on the fifth day he came out and shaved his head, because this was what people did when they came back from the land of the dead.

Afterwards he killed a cow for a great feast. He took the cow's tail and braided it. He decorated it with beads and cowry shells and bits of shiny metal. It was a beautiful thing. Ogaloussa carried it with him to important affairs. When there was a dance or an important ceremony he always had it with him. The people of the village thought it was the most beautiful cow-tail switch they had ever seen.

Soon there was a celebration in the village because Ogaloussa had returned from the dead. The people dressed in their best clothes, the musicians brought out their instruments, and a big dance began. The drummers beat their drums and the women sang. The people drank much palm wine. Everyone was happy.

Ogaloussa carried his cow-tail switch, and everyone admired it. Some of the men grew bold and came forward to Ogaloussa and asked for the cow-tail switch, but Ogaloussa kept it in his hand. Now and then there was a clamor and much confusion as many people asked for it at once. The women and children begged for it too, but Ogaloussa refused them all.

Finally he stood up to talk. The dancing stopped and people came close to hear what Ogaloussa had to say.

"A long time ago I went into the forest," Ogaloussa

said. "While I was hunting I was killed by a leopard. Then my sons came for me. They brought me back from the land of the dead to my village. I will give this cow-tail switch to one of my sons. All of them have done something to bring me back from the dead, but I have only one cow tail to give. I shall give it to the one who did the most to bring me home."

10

So an argument started.

"He will give it to me!" one of the sons said. "It was I who did the most, for I found the trail in the forest when it was lost!"

"No, he will give it to me!" another son said. "It was I who put his bones together!"

"It was I who covered his bones with sinews and flesh!" another said. "He will give it to me!"

"It was I who gave him the power of movement!" another son said. "I deserve it most!"

Another son said it was he who should have the switch, because he had put blood in Ogaloussa's veins. Another claimed it because he had put breath in the body. Each of the sons argued his right to possess the wonderful cow-tail switch.

Before long not only the sons but the other people of the village were talking. Some of them argued that the son who had put blood in Ogaloussa's veins should get the switch, others that the one who had given Ogaloussa's breath should get it. Some of them believed that all of the sons had done equal things, and that they should share it. They argued back and forth this way until Ogaloussa asked them to be quiet.

"To this son I will give the cow-tail switch, for I owe most to him," Ogaloussa said.

He came forward and bent low and handed it to

11

Puli, the little boy who had been born while Ogaloussa was in the forest.

The people of the village remembered then that the child's first words had been, "Where is my father?" They knew that Ogaloussa was right.

For it was a saying among them that a man is not really dead until he is forgotten.

KADDO'S WALL

IN the town of Tendella in the Kingdom of Seno, north of the Gulf of Guinea, there was a rich man by the name of Kaddo. His fields spread out on every side of the town. At plowing time hundreds of men and boys hoed up his fields, and then hundreds of women and girls planted his corn seed in the ground for him. His grain bulged in his granary, because each season he harvested far more than he could use. The name of Kaddo was known far and wide throughout the Kingdom of Seno. Travelers who passed through the town carried tales of his wealth far beyond Seno's borders.

One day Kaddo called all of his people in the town of Tendella together for a big meeting in front of his house. They all came, for Kaddo was an important man, and they knew he was going to make an important announcement.

13

"There's something that bothers me," Kaddo said. "I've been thinking about it for a long time. I've lain awake worrying. I have so much corn in my granary that I don't know what to do with it."

The people listened attentively, and thought about Kaddo's words. Then a man said:

"Some of the people of the town have no corn at all. They are very poor and have nothing. Why don't you give some of your corn to them?"

Kaddo shook his head and said, "No, that isn't a very good idea. It doesn't satisfy me."

Another man said to Kaddo:

"Well, then, you could lend corn to the people who have had a bad harvest and have no seed for the spring planting. That would be very good for the town and would keep poverty away."

"No," Kaddo said, "that's no solution either."

"Well, then, why not sell some of your corn and buy cattle instead?" still another man said.

Kaddo shook his head.

"No, it's not very good advice. It's hard for people to advise a rich man with problems like mine."

Many people made suggestions, but nobody's advice suited Kaddo. He thought for a while, and at last he said:

"Send me as many young girls as you can find. I will have them grind the corn for me."

The people went away. They were angry with Kaddo. But the next day they sent a hundred girls to work for him as he had asked. On a hundred grindstones they began to grind Kaddo's corn into flour. All day long they put corn into the grindstones and took flour out. All day long the people of the town heard the sound of the grinding at Kaddo's house. A pile of corn flour began to grow. For seven days and seven nights the girls ground corn without a pause.

When the last grain of corn was ground into flour, Kaddo called the girls together and said:

"Now bring water from the spring. We shall mix it with the corn flour to make mortar out of it."

So the girls brought water in water pots and mixed it with the flour to make a thick mortar. Then Kaddo

15

ordered them to make bricks out of the mortar.

"When the bricks are dry, then I shall make a wall of them around my house," he said.

Word went out that Kaddo was preparing to build a wall of flour around his house, and the people of the town came to his door and protested.

"You can't do a thing like this, it is against humanity!" they said.

"It's not right, people have no right to build walls with food!" a man said.

"Ah, what is right and what is wrong?" Kaddo said. "My right is different from yours, because I am so very rich. So leave me alone."

"Corn is to eat, so that you may keep alive," another said. "It's not meant to taunt those who are less fortunate."

"When people are hungry it is an affront to shut them out with a wall of flour," another man said.

"Stop your complaints," Kaddo said. "The corn is mine. It is my surplus. I can't eat it all. It comes from my own fields. I am rich. What good is it to be rich if you can't do what you want with your own property?"

The people of the town went away, shaking their heads in anger over Kaddo's madness. The hundred girls continued to make bricks of flour, which they dried in the sun. And when the bricks were dry Kaddo had them begin building the wall around his house. They used wet dough for mortar to hold the bricks together, and slowly the wall grew. They stuck cowry shells into the wall to make beautiful designs, and when at last the wall was done, and the last corn flour used up, Kaddo was very proud. He walked back and forth and looked at his wall. He walked around it. He went in and out of the gate. He was very happy.

And now when people came to see him they had to stand by the gate until he asked them to enter. When the workers who plowed and planted for Kaddo wanted to talk to him, Kaddo sat on the wall by the gate and listened to them and gave them orders. And whenever the people of the town wanted his opinion on an important matter he sat on his wall and gave it to them, while they stood and listened.

Things went on like this for a long time. Kaddo enjoyed his reputation as the richest man for miles around. The story of Kaddo's wall went to the farthest parts of the kingdom.

And then one year there was a bad harvest for Kaddo. There wasn't enough rain to grow the corn, and the earth dried up hard and dusty like the road. There wasn't a single ear of corn in all of Kaddo's fields or the fields of his relatives.

The next year it was the same. Kaddo had no seed corn left, so he sold his cattle and horses to buy corn for food and seed for a new planting. He sowed corn again, but the next harvest time it was the same, and there wasn't a single ear of corn on all his fields.

Year after year Kaddo's crops failed. Some of his relatives died of hunger, and others went away to other parts of the Kingdom of Seno, for they had no more seed corn to plant and they couldn't count on Kaddo's help. Kaddo's workers ran away, because he was unable to feed them. Gradually Kaddo's part of the town became deserted. All that he had left were a young daughter and a mangy donkey.

When his cattle and his money were all gone, Kaddo became very hungry. He scraped away a little bit of the flour wall and ate it. Next day he scraped away more of the flour wall and ate it. The wall got lower and lower. Little by little it disappeared. A day came when the wall was gone, when nothing was left of the elegant structure Kaddo had built around his house, and on which he had used to sit to listen to the people of the town when they came to ask him to lend them a little seed corn.

Then Kaddo realized that if he was to live any longer he must get help from somewhere. He wondered who would help him. Not the people of Tendella, for he had insulted and mistreated them and they would have nothing to do with him. There was only one man he could go to, Sogole, king of the Ganna people, who had the reputation of being very rich and generous.

So Kaddo and his daughter got on the mangy, underfed donkey and rode seven days until they arrived in the land of the Ganna.

Sogole sat before his royal house when Kaddo arrived. He had a soft skin put on the ground next to him for Kaddo to sit upon, and had millet beer brought for the two of them to drink.

"Well, stranger in the land of the Ganna, take a long drink, for you have a long trip behind you if you come from Tendella," Sogole said.

"Thank you, but I can't drink much," Kaddo said.

"Why is that?" Sogole said. "When people are thirsty they drink."

"That is true," Kaddo replied. "But I have been hungry too long, and my stomach is shrunk."

"Well, drink in peace then, because now that you are my guest you won't be hungry. You shall have whatever you need from me."

19

Kaddo nodded his head solemnly and drank a little of the millet beer.

"And now tell me," Sogole said. "You say you come from the town of Tendella in the Kingdom of Seno? I've heard many tales of that town. The famine came there and drove out many people, because they had no corn left."

"Yes," Kaddo said. "Hard times drove them out, and the corn was all gone."

"But tell me, there was a rich and powerful man in Tendella named Kaddo, wasn't there? What ever happened to him? Is he still alive?"

"Yes, he is still alive," Kaddo said.

"A fabulous man, this Kaddo," Sogole said. "They say he built a wall of flour around his house out of his surplus crops, and when he talked to his people he sat on the wall by his gate. Is this true?"

"Yes, it is true," Kaddo said sadly.

"Does he still have as many cattle as he used to?" Sogole asked.

"No, they are all gone."

"It is an unhappy thing for a man who owned so much to come to so little," Sogole said. "But doesn't he have many servants and workers still?"

"His workers and servants are all gone," Kaddo said. "Of all his great household he has only one

20

daughter left. The rest went away because there was no money and no food."

Sogole looked melancholy.

"Ah, what is a rich man when his cattle are gone and his servants have left him? But tell me, what happened to the wall of flour that he built around his house?"

"He ate the wall," Kaddo said. "Each day he scraped a little of the flour from the wall, until it was all gone."

"A strange story," Sogole said. "But such is life."

And he thought quietly for a while about the way life goes for people sometimes, and then he asked:

"And were you, by any chance, one of Kaddo's family?"

"Indeed I was one of Kaddo's family. Once I was rich. Once I had more cattle than I could count. Once I had many cornfields. Once I had hundreds of workers cultivating my crops. Once I had a bursting granary. Once I was Kaddo, the great personage of Tendella."

"What! You yourself are Kaddo?"

"Yes, once I was proud and lordly, and now I sit in rags begging for help."

"What can I do for you?" Sogole asked.

"I have nothing left now. Give me some seed corn,

22

so that I can go back and plant my fields again."

"Take what you need," Sogole said. He ordered his servants to bring bags of corn and to load them on Kaddo's donkey. Kaddo thanked him humbly, and he and his daughter started their return trip to Tendella. They traveled for seven days. On the way Kaddo became very hungry. He hadn't seen so much corn for a long time as he was bringing back from the Kingdom of the Ganna. He took a few grains and put them in his mouth and chewed them. Once more he put a few grains in his mouth. Then he put a whole handful in his mouth and swallowed. He couldn't stop. He ate and ate. He forgot that this was the corn with which he had to plant his fields. When he arrived in Tendella he went to his bed to sleep, and when he arose the next morning he ate again. He ate so much of the corn that he became sick. He went to his bed again and cried out in pain, because his stomach had forgotten what to do with food. And before long Kaddo died.

Kaddo's grandchildren and great-grandchildren in the Kingdom of Seno are poor to this day. And to the rich men of the country the common people sometimes say:

"Don't build a wall of flour around your house."

TALK

ONCE, not far from the city of Accra on the Gulf of Guinea, a country man went out to his garden to dig up some yams to take to market. While he was digging, one of the yams said to him:

"Well, at last you're here. You never weeded me, but now you come around with your digging stick. Go away and leave me alone!"

The farmer turned around and looked at his cow in amazement. The cow was chewing her cud and looking at him.

"Did you say something?" he asked.

The cow kept on chewing and said nothing, but the man's dog spoke up.

"It wasn't the cow who spoke to you," the dog said. "It was the yam. The yam says leave him alone."

The man became angry, because his dog had never talked before, and he didn't like his tone besides. So he took his knife and cut a branch from a palm tree to whip his dog. Just then the palm tree said:

"Put that branch down!"

The man was getting very upset about the way things were going, and he started to throw the palm branch away, but the palm branch said:

"Man, put me down softly!"

He put the branch down gently on a stone, and the stone said:

"Hey, take that thing off me!"

This was enough, and the frightened farmer started to run for his village. On the way he met a fisherman going the other way with a fish trap on his head.

"What's the hurry?" the fisherman asked.

"My yam said, 'Leave me alone!' Then the dog said, 'Listen to what the yam says!' When I went to whip the dog with a palm branch the tree said, 'Put that branch down!' Then the palm branch said, 'Do it softly!' Then the stone said, 'Take that thing off me!'"

"Is that all?" the man with the fish trap asked. "Is that so frightening?"

"Well," the man's fish trap said, "did he take it off the stone?"

"Wah!" the fisherman shouted. He threw the fish trap on the ground and began to run with the farmer, and on the trail they met a weaver with a bundle of cloth on his head.

"Where are you going in such a rush?" he asked them.

"My yam said, 'Leave me alone!'" the farmer said. "The dog said, 'Listen to what the yam says!' The tree said, 'Put that branch down!' The branch said, 'Do it softly!' And the stone said, 'Take that thing off me!'"

"And then," the fisherman continued, "the fish trap said, 'Did he take it off?'"

"That's nothing to get excited about," the weaver said, "no reason at all."

"Oh yes it is," his bundle of cloth said. "If it happened to you you'd run too!"

"Wah!" the weaver shouted. He threw his bundle on the trail and started running with the other men.

They came panting to the ford in the river and found a man bathing.

"Are you chasing a gazelle?" he asked them.

The first man said breathlessly:

"My yam talked at me, and it said, 'Leave me alone!' And my dog said, 'Listen to your yam!' And when I cut myself a branch the tree said, 'Put that branch down!' And the branch said, 'Do it softly!' And the stone said, 'Take that thing off me!'"

27

The fisherman panted:

"And my trap said, 'Did he?'"

The weaver wheezed:

"And my bundle of cloth said, 'You'd run too!'"

"Is that why you're running?" the man in the river asked.

"Well, wouldn't you run if you were in their position?" the river said.

The man jumped out of the water and began to run with the others. They ran down the main street of the village to the house of the chief. The chief's servants brought his stool out, and he came and sat on it to listen to their complaints. The men began to recite their troubles.

"I went out to my garden to dig yams," the farmer said, waving his arms. "Then everything began to talk! My yam said, 'Leave me alone!' My dog said, 'Pay attention to your yam!' The tree said, 'Put that branch down!' The branch said, 'Do it softly!' And the stone said, 'Take it off me!'"

"And my fish trap said, 'Well, did he take it off?'" the fisherman said.

"And my cloth said, 'You'd run too!'" the weaver said.

"And the river said the same," the bather said hoarsely, his eyes bulging.

The chief listened to them patiently, but he couldn't refrain from scowling.

"Now this is really a wild story," he said at last. "You'd better all go back to your work before I punish you for disturbing the peace."

So the men went away, and the chief shook his head and mumbled to himself, "Nonsense like that upsets the community."

"Fantastic, isn't it?" his stool said. "Imagine, a talking yam!"

THE ONE YOU DON'T SEE COMING

THE PEOPLE who lived near the edge of the rain forest, in the country along the banks of the Cavally River, often talked about an animal of the forest called the One You Don't See Coming.

They said that all day long he lurked among the shadows of the great trees, waiting for night to fall. Then, when darkness came, he crept forward as silent as a leopard into the villages.

"Our best hunters have tried to capture this animal," they said. "We have set traps on the trails and at the water holes, but it is no use—he is the stealthiest of all the creatures of the forest. Each night he comes prowling among our houses. He is never heard and never seen."

31

"What does this animal do that we should be afraid of him?" the young people asked.

"The One You Don't See Coming is a thief, "the older people said. "He steals everyone's brains and leaves them forgetful of everything until morning comes. One minute people are the way they are here now, talking back and forth. The next minute the One You Don't See Coming creeps upon them and steals their minds. They no longer talk or think, they simply lie motionless and stupid until the sun rises."

"What good are the dogs if they don't hear him and bark?" the children asked.

"They neither hear him nor smell him. When he comes he takes their brains too. The One You Don't See Coming has another name. Some people call him Sleep."

The young hunters talked about this curious animal among themselves, and one day a man named Biafu said:

"What kind of hunters are we if we can't kill the One You Don't See Coming?"

"That's easy enough to say," a hunter named Gunde said. "But where will you find him? Our grandfathers were good hunters and they never caught him."

"I've heard that he leaves no footprints on the

trail," a hunter named Deeba said. "What will you follow?"

"If he really lives in the forest, as the old people say, then we'll find him. We'll get rid of this nuisance once and for all!" Biafu said.

"I'm not afraid," Gunde said.

"I'll go too," Deeba said. "We'll catch this thing called Sleep, the One You Don't See Coming, and put an end to him. Then the old people will praise us and give us gifts."

So Gunde, Deeba, and Biafu took their hunting knives and spears and went deep into the shadows of the forest.

They listened, but they didn't hear Sleep. They searched the ground for footprints, but Sleep had left no footprints. All day they stalked Sleep. They came to a part of the forest where the villagers hardly ever went.

"He must lurk here among the tall ferns," Biafu said.

"I don't see him," Deeba said.

"I don't hear him," Gunde said.

"If there really is such an animal we shall certainly catch him at the water hole," Biafu said.

So they went down through the dense brush and the tall ferns until they came to where the river made its way through the jungle. The banks of the river were marked with the footprints of the gazelle, the antelope, the buffalo, and the leopard.

"We'll wait for him here, and when he comes to drink we shall kill him," Biafu said.

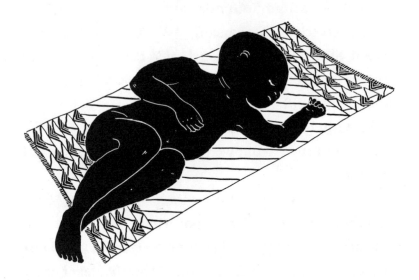

He found a tall tree by the edge of the water. It sloped outward over the river, so that any animal that came to drink would be under its branches.

"Climb the tree," Biafu said to Deeba. "When Sleep comes to drink you can throw yourself upon his back and we will finish him."

Deeba looked up and thought.

"Maybe *you* had better climb the tree," he said to Biafu.

34

"No, Gunde and I will stand guard below, and when we hear you shout we will come running."

Deeba shook his head. So Biafu turned to Gunde and said:

"Then you climb the tree and wait. When Sleep comes to drink you can leap upon him. When we hear you shout, Deeba and I will come running."

Gunde thought a moment. He shook his head too.

"No, I would rather stay on the ground and come running myself."

Biafu became angry.

"What mighty hunters! Afraid of an animal you can't see!"

"Just the same, what if he likes to climb trees?" Deeba said.

"Yes, what if he likes to climb *this* tree?" Gunde said.

They argued and argued. Finally Biafu stamped his foot impatiently.

"All right, I'll climb the tree myself and wait. When you hear me shout, come as fast as you can!" he said. He went up into the branches of the tree overhanging the water and hid among the leaves. Gunde and Deeba crawled into the dense brush and waited.

Time passed. Antelope came down to the water

and drank and went away. Night came, and owls called back and forth. Leopards came silently to drink, and went away. Biafu clung to his tree and watched, his knife held tightly in his hand. Gunde and Deeba crouched in the brush and waited for Biafu to shout.

The misty night grew old, and the moon moved across the sky.

Biafu kept thinking about how pleased the old people would be when they had caught the One You Don't See Coming. But he was very tired. He began to nod. His eyes closed once, just for a short moment. They closed again, just a little longer. Then he was aware that his mind was slipping away into the night. He jerked himself awake, and his heart beat fast, for he knew that the animal was there.

He waved his knife and shouted:

"I see you! I see you!"

Deeba and Gunde ran as fast as they could to the edge of the water.

"Where is he!" they shouted. "Where is he!"

"Ah, he came and then he fled!" Biafu said. "Go back to your hiding place and wait."

Deeba and Gunde went back and crouched in the brush again. Biafu sat up very straight, waiting for the One You Don't See Coming to return. He peered through the darkness at the river. He heard nothing except the owls and the frogs in the distance. The moon moved across the sky.

A great heaviness came over Biafu's mind. No matter how hard he tried to keep them open, his eyes kept closing. For a moment he forgot everything. He seemed to be floating away. The tree swayed in the wind. Biafu clutched at the branches and opened his eyes. He waved his knife in the air and shouted:

"I see you! I see you!"

Again Deeba and Gunde came running, with their spears ready.

"Where is he! Where is he!" they shouted, trying to see in the darkness.

"He is near, he came up in the tree!" Biafu said. "He seized me, but I shook him off! Go back and hide again. Next time we will surely get him. But don't go so far, and run faster when you hear me shout!"

So Deeba and Gunde went back in the brush and waited.

Biafu talked to himself and rubbed his eyes to keep awake. He thought about the big celebration the village would have when he returned from the hunt. A cloud moved slowly across the sky and covered the moon. Things were very dark. There was no wind,

37

and the leaves stopped rustling. The owls in the distance grew silent. The frogs stopped croaking.

And slowly, slowly, Biafu's eyes closed. His memory slipped away into the night. This time Sleep crept slowly upon him. Slowly, slowly, Sleep loosened Biafu's hold on the branches. Slowly Sleep pushed Biafu's head down on his chest. Biafu's knife slipped from his hand and fell into the water below. And slowly, slowly, Sleep pushed him, harder and harder, until he was leaning sideways. And suddenly Sleep seized Biafu and flung him down into the river below.

"Deeba! Gunde! He has me! He has me!" Biafu shouted.

They came running, ready for a great struggle, but they were too late, they only saw Biafu. Sleep was not there.

"Where is he! Where is he!" they shouted as Biafu came dripping out of the water.

"He climbed into the tree, and he threw me into the water!" Biafu said.

He sat down unhappily by the edge of the river and began to think. He was silent a long time, and then he said to Deeba and Gunde:

"It's no use hunting Sleep. The old people are right. And anyway, he's not like the leopard, who steals our goats and doesn't bring them back. What

Sleep steals he steals just for a few hours, and when morning comes you are whole again."

So the hunters took their weapons and hunted an antelope, and they carried it back to the village for a feast. The old people were glad, but they asked about Sleep.

"We almost saw him," Deeba said.

"I wrestled with him in a tree," Biafu said, "but I couldn't hold him."

"He threw Biafu into the river," Gunde said.

"It's the way I've always said," Biafu said with dignity. "You can't see the coming of Sleep. You almost see him but you never do."

KASSA,
THE STRONG ONE

ONCE among the Mende people there was a strong young man named Kassa Kena Genanina.

"I am a strong man," he said, "the strongest man alive, and I'm not afraid of anything!"

One day Kassa went hunting in the forest with two other young men named Iri Ba Farra and Congo Li Ba Jelema. Iri and Congo carried guns to hunt with, but Kassa carried a pole of forged iron.

Iri and Congo hunted and hunted, but they found no game. Kassa, who was swift as well as strong, killed twenty large antelopes with his iron pole, and he brought them into the clearing where Iri and Congo waited.

"Here is the meat," Kassa said. "Now who will go into the forest to get firewood?"

But both Iri and Congo were afraid to go into the forest alone, so Kassa said to Iri:

"You stay and guard the meat so that it won't be stolen by the animals of the jungle. Congo and I will get the firewood."

Kassa and Congo went into the forest, and Iri was alone. And while he watched, a huge bird came flying down from the sky and said to him:

"I am hungry. Shall I take you or shall I take the meat?"

The huge bird was frightening, and Iri said: "By all means take the meat!"

The bird took one of the antelopes and flew off with it. When Kassa and Congo came back Iri said:

"While you were gone a huge bird came down and said, 'Shall I take you or the meat?' I said, 'Take the meat!'"

Kassa was scornful.

"You shouldn't have given him an antelope. You should have said, 'Take me!' "

The next day Kassa went again into the forest to get firewood, and this time he took Iri with him and left Congo to guard the meat.

And when they were gone the huge bird came sailing down from the sky again and said to Congo Li Ba Jelema:

"I am hungry. Shall I take you or the meat?"

Congo was frightened, and he said: "If you're that hungry, then take the meat!"

The bird took one of the antelopes and flew away. When Iri and Kassa returned from the forest Congo told them what had happened.

"The huge bird came back and said, 'Shall I take you or the meat?' And I said, 'Take the meat!' "

Kassa said, "You shouldn't have said that, you should have said, 'Take me.' Tomorrow I shall stay and guard the meat."

So the next day Iri and Congo went together into the forest for firewood, and after they were gone the huge bird sailed down to the clearing and said to Kassa:

"I am hungry. Shall I take you or the meat?"

Kassa sprang up.

43

"I am Kassa Kena Genanina, the strongest man alive!" he shouted. "You shall take nothing, neither the meat nor me!" He seized his forged iron pole and threw it at the bird. It struck her as she flew, and she fell dead upon the ground.

But a tiny feather came loose and floated in the air. It floated downward gently and settled upon Kassa's

shoulders. It was heavy. It pushed him to the ground. He lay upon his stomach, and the feather was still on him, and it was so heavy he couldn't move. He struggled to get up, but the feather held him to the earth.

After a long while a woman carrying a child on her back came by, and Kassa said to her:

"Call my comrades from the forest so they can help me!"

She went into the forest and found Iri and Congo, and they came running to where Kassa lay. First

44

Congo tried to lift the feather from Kassa, then Iri tried, but it was too heavy. Then they tried together, but they couldn't budge it.

The woman stood watching them. Finally she bent forward and blew the feather off Kassa's shoulders with her mouth.

Then she picked up the dead bird from the ground and gave it to the child on her back for a toy, and went away.

ANANSI'S FISHING EXPEDITION

IN the country of Ashanti, not far from the edge of the great West African forest, there was a man named Anansi, who was known to all the people for miles around. Anansi was not a great hunter, or a great worker, or a great warrior. His specialty was being clever. He liked to outwit people. He liked to live well, and to have other people do things for him. But because all the people of the country knew about Anansi and had had trouble with him he had to keep thinking of new ways to get something for nothing.

One day Anansi was sitting in the village when a man named Osansa came along.

"I have an idea," Anansi said. "Why don't we go

47

and set fish traps together? Then we shall sell the fish and be quite rich."

But Osansa knew Anansi's reputation very well, and so he said:

"No, I have as much food as I can eat or sell. I am rich enough. Why don't you set your fish traps by yourself?"

"Ha! Fish alone? Then I'd have to do all the work!" Anansi said. "What I need is a fool for a partner."

Osansa went away, and after a while another man named Anene came along.

"I have an idea," Anansi said. "Why don't the two of us go and set fish traps together? Then we shall sell the fish and be quite rich."

Anene knew Anansi very well too, but he seemed to listen thoughtfully.

"That sounds like a fine idea," he said. "Two people can catch more fish than one. Yes, I'll do it."

The news went rapidly around the village that Anansi and Anene were going on a fishing expedition together. Osansa met Anene in the market and said:

"We hear you are going to trap fish with Anansi. Don't you know he is trying to make a fool of you? He has told everyone that he needs a fool to go fishing with him. He wants someone to set the fish traps

48

and do all the work, while he gets all the money for the fish."

"Don't worry, friend Osansa, I won't be Anansi's fool," Anene said.

Early the next morning Anansi and Anene went into the woods to cut palm branches to make their fish traps.

Anansi was busy thinking how he could make Anene do most of the work. But when they came to the place where the palm trees grew, Anene said to Anansi:

"Give me the knife, Anansi. I shall cut the branches

for the traps. We are partners. We share everything. My part of the work will be to cut branches, your part of the work will be to get tired for me."

"Just a minute, let me think," Anansi said. "Why should I be the one to get tired?"

"Well, when there's work to be done someone must get tired," Anene said. "That's the way it is. So if I cut the branches the least you can do is to get tired for me."

"Hah, you take me for a fool?" Anansi said. "Give me the knife. I shall cut the branches and *you* get tired for *me !*"

So Anansi took the knife and began cutting the branches from the trees. Every time he chopped, Anene grunted. Anene sat down in the shade and groaned from weariness, while Anansi chopped and hacked and sweated. Finally the wood for the fish traps was cut. Anansi tied it up into a big bundle. Anene got up from the ground holding his back and moaning.

"Anansi, let me carry the bundle of wood now, and you can get tired for me," Anene said.

"Oh, no, my friend Anene," Anansi said, "I am not that simple minded. I'll carry the wood myself, and you can take the weariness for me."

So he hoisted the bundle to the top of his head and

the two of them started back to the village. Anene groaned all the way.

"Oh, oh!" he moaned. "Take it easy, Anansi! Oh, oh!"

When they came to the village Anene said:

"Let me make the fish traps, Anansi, and you just sit down and get tired for me."

"Oh, no," Anansi said. "You just keep on as you are." And he made the fish traps while Anene lay on his back in the shade with his eyes closed, moaning and groaning.

And while he was making the traps, working in the heat with perspiration running down his face and chest, Anansi looked at Anene lying there taking all his weariness and sore muscles for him, and he shook his head and clucked his tongue.

"Anene thinks he is intelligent," he said to himself. "Yet look at him moaning and groaning there, practically dying from weariness!"

When the fish traps were done Anene climbed to his feet and said, "Anansi, my friend, now let me carry the fish traps to the water, and you can get tired for me."

"Oh, no," Anansi said. "You just come along and do your share. I'll do the carrying, you do the getting-tired."

51

So they went down to the water, Anansi carrying and Anene moaning. When they arrived, Anene said to Anansi:

"Now wait a minute, Anansi, we ought to think things over here. There are sharks in this water. Someone is apt to get hurt. So let me go in and set the traps, and should a shark bite me, then you can die for me."

"Wah!" Anansi howled. "Listen to that! What do you take me for? I'll go in the water and set the traps myself, and if I am bitten, then *you* can die for *me!*" So he took the fish traps out into the water and set

52

them, and then the two of them went back to the village.

The next morning when they went down to inspect the traps they found just four fish. Anene spoke first.

"Anansi, there are only four fish here. You take them. Tomorrow there will probably be more, and then I'll take my turn."

"Now, what do you take me for?" Anansi said indignantly. "Do you think I am simple-minded? Oh, no, Anene, you take the four fish and I'll take my turn tomorrow."

So Anene took the four fish and carried them to town and sold them.

Next day when they came down to the fish traps, Anene said:

"Look, there are only eight fish here. I'm glad it's your turn, because tomorrow there doubtless will be more."

"Just a minute," Anansi said. "You want me to take today's fish so that tomorrow you get a bigger catch? Oh no, these are all yours, partner, tomorrow I'll take my share."

So Anene took the eight fish and carried them to town and sold them.

Next day when they came to look in the traps they found sixteen fish.

"Anansi," Anene said, "take the sixteen fish. Little ones, too. I'll take my turn tomorrow."

"Of course you'll take your turn tomorrow, it's my turn today," Anansi said. He stopped to think. "Well, now, you are trying to make a fool out of me again! You want me to take these sixteen miserable little fish so that you can get the big catch tomorrow, don't you? Well, it's a good thing I'm alert! You take the sixteen today and I'll take the big catch tomorrow!"

So Anene carried the sixteen fish to the market and sold them.

Next day they came to the traps and took the fish out. But by this time the traps had rotted in the water.

"Well, it's certainly your turn today," Anene said. "And I'm very glad of that. Look, the fish traps are rotten and worn out. We can't use them any more. I'll tell you what—you take the fish to town and sell them, and I'll take the rotten fish traps and sell them. The fish traps will bring an excellent price. What a wonderful idea!"

"Hm," Anansi said. "Just a moment, don't be in such a hurry. I'll take the fish traps and sell them myself. If there's such a good price to be had, why shouldn't I get it instead of you? Oh, no, *you* take the fish, my friend."

Anansi hoisted the rotten fish traps up on his head

54

and started off for town. Anene followed him, carrying the fish. When they arrived in the town Anene sold his fish in the market, while Anansi walked back and forth singing loudly:

"I am selling rotten fish traps! I am selling wonderful rotten fish traps!"

But no one wanted rotten fish traps, and the townspeople were angry that Anansi thought they were so stupid they would buy them. All day long Anansi wandered through the town singing:

"Get your rotten fish traps here! I am selling wonderful rotten fish traps!"

Finally the head man of the town heard about the

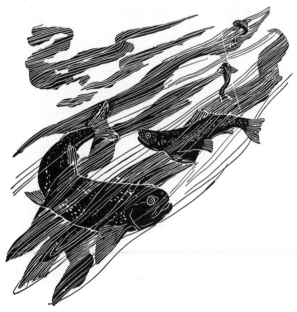

affair. He too became very angry, and he sent messengers for Anansi. When they brought Anansi to him he asked indignantly:

"What do you think you are doing, anyway? What kind of nonsense is this you are trying to put over the people of the town?"

"I'm selling rotten fish traps," Anansi said, "very excellent rotten fish traps."

"Now what do you take us for?" the chief of the town said. "Do you think we are ignorant people? Your friend Anene came and sold good fish, which the people want, but you come trying to sell something that isn't good for anything and just smell the town up with your rotten fish traps. It's an outrage. You insult us."

The head man turned to the townspeople who stood near by, listening.

"Take him away and whip him," he said.

The men took Anansi out to the town gate and beat him with sticks. Anansi shouted and yelled and made a great noise. When at last they turned him loose, Anene said to him:

"Anansi, this ought to be a lesson to you. You wanted a fool to go fishing with you, but you didn't have to look so hard to find one. You were a fool yourself."

Anansi nodded his head.

"Yes," he said thoughtfully, rubbing his back and his legs where they had beat him. And he looked reproachfully at Anene. "But what kind of partner are you? At least you could have taken the pain while I took the beating."

YOUNDE
GOES TO TOWN

ONCE in the country of Akim, in the hills far back
from the coast, there was a man named Younde. He
was a simple man who had never been far from home,
and he spent his time at farming and hunting like the
other people of the village. He had often heard talk
about the big town of Accra by the ocean, and all the·
wonderful things to be found there, but he had never
seen it. He had never been farther from his village
than the river.

But one day Younde had to go to Accra. He put on
his best clothes, and took his knife and put it in his
belt. He wrapped some food in a cloth and put it on
his head and started out. He walked for many days,
and the road was hot and dusty. After a while he was
out of his own country, and people didn't speak
Akim, which was his language, any more. He came

closer and closer to Accra. There were many people and donkeys on the way, all going to town or coming back from town, more people than he had ever seen on the road before.

Then he saw a great herd of cows grazing by the edge of the road. He had never seen so many cows in his life. He stopped and looked at them in wonder. He saw a little boy herding the cows and he went up to him and said, "Who is the owner of all these cattle?"

But the boy didn't understand Younde, because Younde spoke Akim, while in Accra they spoke the Ga language, and he replied, "Minu," which meant "I don't understand."

"Minu! What a rich man he must be to own so many cows!" Younde said.

He continued his way into the town. He was very impressed with everything he saw.

He came to a large building and stopped to look at it. It was made of stone, and it was very high. He shook his head. There was nothing like this back in the hills. When a woman came by on her way to market Younde spoke to her.

"What a tremendous house!" he said. "What rich person can own such a building?"

But the woman didn't know what Younde was saying, because he talked Akim and she knew only Ga, so she replied to him:

"Minu."

"Minu! That man again!"

Younde was overcome. No one back in Akim had ever been so wealthy as Minu. As he went farther and farther into the town he kept seeing more wonders. He came to the market. It covered a space larger than all the houses in Younde's village. He walked through the center of it, and saw the women selling things that were rare in his village, like iron pots and iron spoons.

"Where do all these things come from?" Younde asked a little girl.

She smiled at him.

"Minu," she replied.

Younde was silent. Everything was Minu. Minu everywhere.

The crowd was very great. People pushed and shoved, for it was the big market day and everyone within walking distance had come to sell or buy. Younde had never seen so many people in one place. The stories he had heard about Accra hadn't done it justice. He stopped an old man with a drum under his arm and said:

"So many people, all at one time! What makes so many people all come to Accra?"

"Minu," the old man said.

Younde was overwhelmed. What influence that Minu had! People came to Accra in great crowds just because of him. How ignorant folks back in the village were of this great personage.

He went out of the market down to the ocean's edge. Lying in the water were many little fishing boats with sails, the first Younde had ever seen.

"Wah! To whom do all those boats belong?" he asked a fisherman standing on the beach.

"Minu," the fisherman replied.

Younde walked away, and came to where a large iron cargo ship was being loaded with palm oil and fruit. Smoke came out of its stacks in huge black clouds, and hundreds of men swarmed over its decks.

"Hah!" Younde said in great excitement to a man

carrying a stalk of bananas on his head. "This must be the largest boat in the world!"

"Minu," the man said.

"Yes, I know, that much I guessed," Younde said. "But where is all the fruit going?"

"Minu," the man said, and went up onto the deck of the ship.

Younde was overcome. Minu was indeed a great man. He owned everything. He ate everything. You couldn't ask a question but what people would answer "Minu." Minu here, there, everywhere.

"I wouldn't have believed it if I hadn't seen it," Younde said. "They ought to call Accra 'Minu's Town.' How wonderful it would be to have Minu's great wealth!"

Younde then transacted his business in Accra, and again he wrapped food in his cloth and set it on his head and started out for home.

When he came to the edge of the town he saw a great procession and heard the beating of drums. He came close and saw it was a funeral. Men were carrying a coffin and women were crying out in mourning. It was the most impressive funeral Younde had ever seen. He pushed his way into the crowd and looked. And to one of the mourners he said:

"Who is this person who has died?"

63

And the mourner replied sadly:

"Minu."

"What! The great Minu is dead?" Younde said. "The man who owned the cattle and the tall house, the sailing boats and the iron steamship? The man whose reputation has crowded the market place beyond belief? Oh, poor Minu! He had to leave all his wealth behind. He has died just like an ordinary person!"

Younde continued his way out of the city, but he couldn't get the tragedy of Minu from his mind.

"Poor Minu!" he said over and over again. "Poor Minu!"

THE
SINGING TORTOISE

FAR BACK in the country, near where the Adiri
River comes out of the Kong Mountains, a hunter
named Ama left his village one day to go hunting.
Game was hard to find, and he went deeper and
deeper into the forest looking for it. He came to the
edge of the river in a part of the forest he had never
seen before, and while he stood thinking where to go
he heard music coming from among the trees. He
heard a voice singing, and the faint tinkling of a *sansa*, which is a kind of tiny piano played with the
thumbs. The voice was singing:

"It is man who imposes himself upon things,
Not things which impose themselves upon man."

Ama moved forward quietly and peered through the trees, and there, sitting in a little clearing in the forest, was a tortoise with a *sansa* in her hands. She sang:

"It is man who imposes himself upon things,
Not things which impose themselves upon man."

Ama was astounded. The tortoise sang beautifully. Never had such a thing been heard of in his country. He stood and listened. The tortoise was not afraid but continued to sing and play. The music was as entrancing as anything Ama had ever heard.

He went back to his village after a while, but he couldn't forget the tortoise. The next time he went hunting in the forest he made his way again to the clearing, and there again he found the tortoise with her *sansa* and heard her sing:

"It is man who imposes himself upon things,
Not things which impose themselves upon man."

Every time that Ama was in the forest he went to hear the tortoise, for she was a strange and wonderful thing. And then one day he thought how fine it would be if he had the tortoise in his house in the village, so that he could hear her sing at night when he came home from hunting or working his fields. He spoke to the tortoise and asked her if he might take her back with him.

"But this thing is a secret," the tortoise said. "If you took me back with you people would get to know about it."

"No," Ama said, "if I had you in my house I would tell no one. It is only I who would hear you."

"If that is true I'll go back with you," the tortoise said. "But I shall sing only for you, and the people of your village mustn't know."

"No," Ama said happily, "you shall sing just for me!"

He picked the tortoise up with great care so that he wouldn't hurt her, and carried her back to his house. And there each night when Ama came in from the fields or from the hunt the tortoise played her *sansa* and sang to him.

Yet it was such a wonderful thing that Ama couldn't keep from speaking about it to people in the village. He talked about it more and more. Among themselves the people ridiculed Ama for telling such a fantastic tale. No one really believed him. The story of Ama's singing tortoise spread farther and farther, and one day it reached the ears of the chief.

"Who is this man who pretends to have a singing tortoise?" the chief said. "He will bring ridicule upon us with this silly story." And the chief sent messengers to Ama to tell him to come to his house.

When Ama came the chief sat upon his stool in his courtyard, with his councilors standing by, and listened to the tale. Ama felt proud and important to own the thing that was causing so much excitement in the district.

But the chief was disturbed, and the councilors shook their heads and were scornful of what Ama told them.

"There's no such thing as a singing tortoise," they said, "or a tortoise that can play a *sansa*."

"Everything I have told you is the way it happened," Ama said.

"You are impudent," the people said. "You are bringing disgrace upon us with your nonsensical talk."

Ama's feelings were hurt, and he said:

"I'll bring the tortoise here. She will sing and play for you. If she can't do this, then you may beat me for it!"

He went back to his village. Everyone was talking about Ama and his tortoise. He picked her up carefully and started off.

"Where are we going?" the tortoise asked.

"The people think I am lying," Ama said. "We'll show them!" The tortoise said nothing.

When Ama came to the chief's house there was a great crowd around it, for people had come from all the near-by villages to see what would happen. Ama placed the tortoise on the ground and put her *sansa* beside her.

"Now you will see," he said.

The tortoise stayed quietly where Ama had placed her, and the people pushed close in a circle to see. But the tortoise didn't sing, nor did she pick up the *sansa*. The people waited. Nothing happened. The people argued among themselves. They became impatient. Minutes passed by. The tortoise pulled her head into her shell. Sometimes she put her head out to look at the people, and then she would pull it in again. Finally the people became angry.

"Well, when is she going to sing?" they asked.

"Sing for them so they will see I am not a liar," Ama said to the tortoise. But the tortoise only blinked her eyes. Time passed. People began to say angry things to Ama.

At last the chief said, "Well, we have seen. This man Ama has ridiculed us with his story. Now take him and beat him for it."

So the people took Ama where he stood and beat him hard with sticks. They beat him a long time, until the chief told them to stop.

"This will teach you not to bring a bad name to our people by lying," the chief said. "Now pack your things and leave the village, for we have no room for such troublemakers."

Ama said nothing. His body ached and he was overcome with shame. He took his possessions and left the village. The people watched him until he was out of sight.

At this moment the tortoise put her head out of her shell and spoke. The people looked in wonder.

"Ama earned his shame through bad faith," the

70

tortoise said. "He brought his punishment upon himself. I was happy in the forest singing and playing my *sansa*. Then he brought me to his house, promising to keep my secret. But he couldn't keep it. He told it to all the world, first in whispers, then with a loud voice."

Then she picked up her little *sansa* and sang once more:

"It is man who imposes himself upon things,
Not things which impose themselves upon man."

TIME

ONCE there was a rich man in Africa whose name was Time. He owned more goats, chickens, and cattle than he could count. He possessed more land then he had ever seen, and on his farms were grown vast quantities of rice, manioc, and all kinds of foods. He had immense stores of cloth, and his many granaries were always overflowing with grain. His reputation had spread far beyond his own tribe. Traders came from distant towns to do business with Time. Dancers, acrobats, and wrestlers came to perform for him. Tribes far and wide sent messengers just to see Time face to face and to return and tell the people what he looked like, and how he lived. To the strangers who visited him Time gave rich presents of cows, goats, and fine cloth. People said that a man who had not seen Time hadn't really lived.

But Time grew old, and his fortunes changed. His wealth disappeared. His cattle grew fewer and fewer,

7 3

his lands grew small, and his stores of grain shrank to nothing. His well-fed body became lean and starved. His house became dilapidated and uncared for, and Time came to look like the poorest of beggars. Yet in distant countries they didn't know about Time's change of fortune.

One day the people of a tribe far from Time's town appointed a number of messengers to visit him.

"Go to Time's country and see him," the messengers were told. "After you have looked at him come back and tell us if he is as rich and generous as people say."

The messengers set out on their long trip, and walked for many days. When at last they came to the edge of the town where Time lived they met a poor old man, thin and wrinkled, and dressed in rags.

"Man, tell us," they asked him, "does Time live here? And if so, where is his house?"

"Yes, Time lives here," the old man said. "Enter the town and people will show you where to find him."

They went into the town and greeted the townspeople.

"We have come to see Time, whose reputation has spread so far," the messengers said. "We want to meet this wonderful man, so that we can go back to our country and describe him to our people."

While they talked there, the old beggar whom the messengers had seen at the edge of the town came walking toward them.

"Time, the man for whom you have been looking, is coming now," someone said.

The visitors looked, and when they saw Time they were very dejected.

"Can this be the man whose name is known even in our country?" they asked. They couldn't believe it, for this beggar was the poorest of all poor people. Never had they seen a man looking so miserable.

When Time came to where they were sitting they shook hands with him and asked:

"Man, are you really Time, of whom everyone has heard?"

"Yes," he said, "I am Time."

"But how can that be? We listened and listened to stories about Time in our country. Travelers came with great tales about his fabulous wealth and influence. Our people sent us here to see him, so that we could return and tell them about Time."

"Well, I am Time. My fortunes have changed," Time said. "I was once the richest man in the world, and now I am the poorest."

"Well, then, that's the way it is," they said sadly. "But whatever shall we tell our people now?"

Time thought for a while, and then he said to them:

"When you get to your country once more and see your people, tell them this: 'Behold, Time isn't what it used to be!'"

THE MESSENGER
TO MAFTAM

AMONG the Soninke people, many days· on foot north of the Gulf of Guinea, there lived a man by the· name of Mamadi. He was poor, and lived in a small and unpretentious house. Yet Mamadi was much respected everywhere because it was said that he never told a falsehood, no matter how small.

One day Bahene, chief of the Soninke, after having heard a long conversation about Mamadi, said in an irritated way:

"Who is this man Mamadi who is so full of virtue and cleverness that he never makes a false statement?"

"He lives in the small village of Ogo," his councilors told him. "He is known far and wide, because he never says a thing that isn't so."

"I believe this character is an exaggeration," the chief said. "There is no such man, either in the desert or the plains. Have him brought here for me to see."

So the messengers brought Mamadi to the chief, and Bahene said to him:

"Mamadi, is it true that you have never lied?"

"Yes, it is true," Mamadi said.

"It is hard to believe," Bahene said. "There is no one alive who hasn't at some time or other said something that wasn't strictly so. Yet, the people say it is true. But tell me, are you certain that you won't ever tell an untruth?"

"Yes, I am quite certain," Mamadi answered.

"How can one be so sure of such a thing?" Bahene asked. "Isn't it presumptuous to say in advance what one will do, without even considering the circumstances?"

"The circumstances are quite unimportant," Mamadi said, "for I am unable to say what is false."

"Well, you seem to be a virtuous man," Bahene said. "If your tongue is as faithful to your principles as you say, then I'm wrong in thinking there is no man who doesn't lie. But if you do lie, then you will commit an act more offensive than when an ordinary person lies, because the ordinary person makes no such virtue of his tongue. So take care, Mamadi, for the day you do tell a lie will be a bad one for you. If the Soninke people ever catch you in a falsehood, I'll have you beaten with ropes!''

When Mamadi had gone back to his village, Bahene said to his councilors:

"That village man is putting on airs! He must have some virtue, since his reputation is widespread. But it requires more than virtue to tell no falsehoods, it takes cleverness as well. Mamadi's certainty that he can't tell a lie is arrogant. He needs a lesson!''

Early one morning, several days later, Bahene sent for Mamadi again. The village man arrived before Bahene's house to find him and his men standing with their weapons in their hands.

"Mamadi, I need you to do a service for me. Please go to my other house in the village of Maftam to deliver a message to my wife. Tell her that we have gone hunting for antelope, and that we shall arrive at Maftam today at noon. We shall be very hungry and shall want plenty to eat. Wait there, and you will eat with us."

Bahene and his hunters started out as though to hunt, while Mamadi took the trail to Maftam, hurrying so that he would get the message there in time for the chief's wife to prepare food. But as soon as Mamadi was out of sight, Bahene turned around and went back to his house. He put down his weapons, and said to the men in his hunting party:

"Well, I have changed my mind! We won't go hunting after all. Nor will we go to Maftam today. This country fellow Mamadi who carries the message to my wife believes that he can't tell an untruth. We'll see. He will tell my wife that we are hunting and that we are going to bring an antelope. He will tell her that we shall arrive at noon, and that we will be very hungry. But none of these things will happen. When we finally get there we shall have a great laugh, for the poor villager's wisdom isn't as great as his

virtue. And then Mamadi shall be beaten for his arrogance."

Mamadi hurried to Maftam. It was three hours away on foot. When he arrived he went to Bahene's wife and said to her:

"I am carrying an urgent message from Bahene."

"What is it?" she asked him.

"Of that I am not sure," Mamadi said.

"How can you carry a message of which you aren't sure?"

Bahene's wife was getting angry.

"What are you supposed to tell me?"

"It is likely, rather, or so it seemed, perhaps, possibly, or, on the other hand more or less certainly, probably less than more, or more than less, that Bahene went hunting."

"It's not very clear," Bahene's wife said. "Did he or didn't he?"

"It's the way I said," Mamadi went on. "When I saw him and the hunters they were clearly going hunting. I could tell by the way they stood around with their weapons in their hands. Yet of course people sometimes stand around like that when they have just returned from the hunt. It's not likely that they just returned from the hunt, though, because there wasn't any meat, but of course they could have hunted and not found any game, so I suppose they were going hunting instead of coming back, more or less, to be sure, somewhat, none the less, however, or at least that was the general impression that was to be gained from the conversation, which was fairly explicit, in a way . . . "

"Try not to get excited," Bahene's wife said. "I don't yet understand whether he is going hunting or not. But what other news is there?"

"Well, it would be wise to be prepared to cook an antelope, of some sort, just about, in case they catch one, although certainly that is Bahene's general intention, possibly, most likely, more or less, that is, in the event they have gone hunting."

"Of all the people among the Soninke villages, Bahene had to pick you!" she said in disgust. "What else is there to know, almost?"

"Oh, yes, there won't be much time, it would seem, and Bahene's hunting party will assuredly, in all likelihood, be somewhat, or exceedingly, or conceivably hardly at all, hungry, when they arrive here exactly or approximately at noon, if they do, although it is most probable, and there is no grave doubt that they won't, even though some question arises as to the certainty, of which there could be some doubt, within bounds, probably . . . "

"Wait! Stop a moment!" Bahene's wife cried out. "So far I haven't learned a thing! Is there something more precise you can tell me?"

"Something more?" Mamadi continued. "Oh, yes. I am to wait for him here until he arrives, if that is possible, or even likely, or otherwise . . . "

"Stop your babbling!" Bahene's wife said. "Is he coming or isn't he? And when will he be here?"

"Well, now, as I said before, more or less clearly than I might have, somewhat, or not altogether, it appears, seemingly, though not conclusively, or even assuredly, that Bahene might, at least ought to, sooner or later . . . "

"Never mind!" Bahene's wife interrupted. "Tell me no more! The more you say the less I know!"

Then Mamadi lay down upon a mat to await the chief's arrival. Noon came and went, but Bahene and his hunters didn't appear. Night came, then morning, and finally the chief arrived in Maftam with his following. They all laughed as they saw their messenger waiting for them in the court.

"Well, our meal is perhaps a little spoiled, but no matter," Bahene said, "for we have proved that even a most virtuous man may allow his tongue to speak a lie, and that this man's arrogance is more noteworthy than his virtues."

"How is that?" Bahene's wife asked.

"Why, he told you that we had gone hunting, when we hadn't, and that we would be here yesterday noon, when we weren't, and that we would bring an antelope, which we didn't. So now he is to be beaten as a lesson to him."

"No," the chief's wife said, "he said that you would do this or you wouldn't, that it was likely or unlikely, or certain or uncertain. He delivered the message, but he gave it with so many qualifications and exceptions that I really didn't get any sense out of him at all."

Bahene was crestfallen. It was he, not Mamadi, who was shamed in public. So he had presents given to Mamadi, and said to him:

"I was wrong, Mamadi, and you are, in truth, a virtuous and wise man. I know now what all the other Soninke people already knew, that you will never tell a lie."

"That is quite true," Mamadi replied. "I never never shall, presumably, it is certain, probably . . . "

GUINEA FOWL
AND RABBIT
GET JUSTICE

SOMEWHERE between the Kong Mountains and the sea, in the country of Ghana, the bird named Guinea Fowl had his farm. It was a good farm. Guinea Fowl worked hard on it, and grew fine yams and bananas. He grew beans and okra, millet and tobacco. His farm always looked green and prosperous. Mostly it was because Guinea Fowl was a hard worker. Not very far away Rabbit had a farm. It wasn't a very good farm because Rabbit never worked too hard. He planted at planting time, but he never hoed his crops or pulled out the weeds that grew there. So when harvest time came along there wasn't very much okra or beans or millet.

One day Rabbit was out walking and he saw Guinea Fowl's farm. It looked so much better than his own that he wished he owned it. He thought it over. He became indignant.

"Why is it that it rains over here on Guinea Fowl's land and not on mine, so that his crops grow and mine don't?" he asked himself. "It's not fair!"

He thought all day. And a wonderful idea came to him.

That night he brought out his wife and his children and marched them to Guinea Fowl's farm, then he marched them back again. He did it again. All night his family went back and forth from their house to Guinea Fowl's farm, until by morning they had made a trail. In the morning they started pulling up Guinea Fowl's vegetables and putting them in baskets.

When Guinea Fowl came to work he saw Rabbit there with his family, pulling up all the fine crops he had planted.

"What are you doing with my yams and okra?" Guinea Fowl said. "And what are you doing on my farm, anyway?"

"*Your* farm?" Rabbit said. "There must be some mistake. It's *my* farm."

"I guess there *is* a mistake. It's my farm. I planted it and I weeded it and I hoed it," Guinea Fowl said. "So I don't see how it can be your farm."

"How could you plant it and weed it and hoe it when I planted it and weeded it and hoed it?" Rabbit said.

Guinea Fowl was very angry.

"You'd better get off my place," he said.

"You'd better get off *my* place," Rabbit said.

"It's absurd," Guinea Fowl said.

"It certainly is," Rabbit said, "when any old Guinea Fowl can come and claim someone else's property."

"It's mine," Guinea Fowl said.

"It's mine," Rabbit said.

"Well, I'll take the case to the chief," Guinea Fowl said.

"It's a good idea," Rabbit said.

So the two of them picked up their hoes and went to the village to the house of the chief.

"This fellow is pulling up

my vegetables," Guinea Fowl said, "and he won't get off my farm."

"He's trying to take advantage of me," Rabbit said. "I work and work to grow fine yams and then he comes along and wants to own them."

They argued and argued, while the head man listened. Finally they went out together to look the situation over.

"Where is the trail from your house?" the head man asked Rabbit.

"There," Rabbit said, and pointed out the one he had just made.

"And where is the trail from your house?" the head man asked Guinea Fowl.

"Trail? I never had a trail," Guinea Fowl said.

"Whenever anyone has a farm he has a trail to it from his house," the head man said.

"But whenever I come to work my farm I *fly*," Guinea Fowl said.

The head man thought. He shook his head.

"If a person has a farm he has to have a trail to it," he said after a while. "So the land must belong to Rabbit."

He went away. Rabbit and his family began to pull up more yams. Guinea Fowl went home, feeling very angry.

90

When Rabbit had a large basket full of vegetables he started off to market with them. But the basket was very heavy. He wasn't used to heavy work, because he was lazy. After he had carried his load a little distance along the road he put it down to rest. And while he sat by the roadside Guinea Fowl came along.

"Ah, friend Rabbit, your load is very heavy," Guinea Fowl said sweetly. "Perhaps I can give you a lift with it."

Rabbit was touched. Guinea Fowl wasn't angry any more. He was very friendly.

"Thank you," he said. "You are a real friend to help me with my vegetables."

So Guinea Fowl put the load on his head. He smiled at Rabbit. Then he flapped his wings and went off with the load, not to the market but to his own house.

Rabbit shouted. He ran after Guinea Fowl, but he couldn't catch him. Guinea Fowl soared over the fields and was gone.

Rabbit was angry. He went back to the village to find the head man.

"Guinea Fowl has robbed me!" he shouted. "He flew away with my basket of vegetables!"

The head man sent for Guinea Fowl.

"They were my vegetables I took," Guinea Fowl said.

"They were mine," Rabbit shouted. "I harvested them with my own hands!"

They argued and argued. The head man thought and thought.

"Well," he said at last, "when people carry things a great deal on their heads, after a while the hair gets thin from so much carrying." The people of the village said yes, that always happened.

"Let me see the top of your head," the head man said to Rabbit.

Rabbit showed him. The head man clicked his tongue.

"No," he said to Rabbit, "your hair is thick and long."

He turned to Guinea Fowl.

"Let me see yours," he said, and Guinea Fowl showed him.

Guinea Fowl's head didn't have even a fuzzy feather on it.

"It must belong to you," the head man said, "you are absolutely bald."

"But Guinea Fowl never *had* any feathers on his head!" Rabbit complained. "He was *always* bald!"

"When you carry things on your head the hair becomes thin," the head man said. "So the basket belongs to Guinea Fowl."

They went away. Rabbit prepared another basket of vegetables to take to market. And when he set it down by the side of the road to rest, Guinea Fowl swooped down and took it away. Rabbit prepared another basket, and the same thing happened. It was no use going to the head man any more, because Guinea Fowl's head was so bald.

At last Rabbit got tired of pulling up Guinea Fowl's vegetables for him, and he went back to his own farm to work for himself.

That is why people sometimes say, "The shortest path often goes nowhere."

ANANSI AND NOTHING
GO HUNTING
FOR WIVES

IT came to Anansi one time, as he sat in his little hut, that he needed a wife. For most men this would have been a simple affair, but Anansi's bad name had spread throughout the country and he knew that he wouldn't be likely to have much luck finding a wife in near-by villages. If only he were a rich and important man like Nothing, who lived on the next hill, everything in life would be so much easier. One could see by the way that Nothing walked and talked and wore his fine clothes that he was a man of significance. People said, "Here he comes" when Nothing approached, and listened attentively when he spoke, and said, "There he goes" when he went away. Nothing would have no trouble getting a wife.

One morning Anansi went across the little valley to the hill where Nothing lived and followed the trail up to his house. It was a large clean house with fresh palm thatch on the roof.

"Hello, friend Nothing, I have been thinking about you," Anansi said. "It is a shame that you live all alone with only servants to take care of you. You ought to have a wife."

"That is a good idea, Anansi," Nothing said. "I have been thinking about it myself."

"Well, I have been thinking of going to Komasi to find a wife for myself, and I thought that we might make the trip together," Anansi said. "Then we can both find wives."

"Ah, that's a good idea," Nothing said after a while. "Let's do it."

The next morning Anansi and Nothing met at the crossroads down in the valley and they began the long walk to Komasi. Anansi wore his best cotton clothes, but they weren't very good because he didn't work very hard and affairs never went very well for him. Nothing wore cotton too, but his clothes were fine and full of beautiful colors.

"If I were dressed like Nothing," Anansi said to

96

himself, "I would make a great impression in Komasi."

After a while he said to Nothing:

"My friend, just for the fun of it let's change shirts for a while."

Nothing was amused by the idea, and the two men changed shirts. An hour or so later Anansi said:

"Friend Nothing, just to entertain ourselves on this long trip let's change coats for a while, just until we get to Komasi."

Nothing laughed at the idea, and the two of them changed coats.

"Now you look like Nothing and I look like Anansi," Nothing said. Anansi felt very proud, looking like Nothing.

Finally they came to Komasi.

"Oh, I have a message to take to my uncle," Anansi said suddenly. "I'll meet you later." And he disappeared down one of the streets of Komasi without stopping to give Nothing's clothes back to him.

"Well, he certainly has urgent business," Nothing said. But Anansi was gone, so Nothing shrugged his shoulders and began to look for a wife.

Anansi was very impressed with himself in Nothing's clothes. He walked like Nothing and talked like Nothing, and people regarded him as a very important personage. When he had been in Komasi only three days he found a beautiful wife, for people were impressed with him.

But Nothing had a hard time of it. He looked like a beggar, and people didn't want to have much to do with him. No man wanted his daughter to marry such an unfortunate character. Yet after a while a poor woman said to Nothing, "Take my daughter, for though you are poor too, you are better off than we are." So Nothing took her. She was not beautiful, like Anansi's wife. But she was the only girl in Komasi that would have him.

The two of them started the long walk back to Nothing's village. On the road they met Anansi, dressed in Nothing's fine clothes, riding on a donkey with his beautiful wife.

"Aha, friend Nothing, there you are!" Anansi said. "I looked for you and looked for you. Where were you keeping yourself? I see you didn't have very good luck."

Nothing looked at Anansi's beautiful young wife and at the donkey they were riding, but he didn't mention the clothes.

When they came to the crossroads both of the wives were surprised. The trail leading to Anansi's place was dirty and overgrown with brush, while the trail leading to Nothing's house was clean and well trimmed. Nothing's servants were waiting for him with water to wash in and fresh clothing.

The two wives were silent. Anansi and Nothing left one another, and each went to his own house.

Anansi's wife found herself in a miserable old hut, and Nothing's wife found herself in a new clean house.

Anansi's wife stood it as long as she could. She was very unhappy. One evening she slipped away and went down the trail to Nothing's house. Nothing's wife was kind to her, and she decided that, as she had been tricked, she wouldn't go back to live with Anansi. She stayed with Nothing and his wife.

But when Anansi learned where his wife had gone he was very angry. He had gone to a lot of trouble and had walked all the way to Komasi to get her. He had even outwitted Nothing to get her, and now she had left him to live with Nothing and his wife.

Anansi decided to kill Nothing. So one night he went out and dug a hole in the trail that came down from Nothing's house. He made the hole very deep, and he put sharp wooden stakes in the bottom, as though he were making a trap to catch an animal. He covered the hole with small limbs and leaves to hide it, and he smeared the trail with grease to make it slippery. Then he hid in the brush and shouted:

"Friend Nothing, come at once, I must see you!"

Nothing's wife said, "Don't go to Anansi, he is a bad character."

Anansi's wife who had run away from him said, "Anansi is a trickster. You can't believe him, so don't go down the trail in the dark."

But Anansi kept calling, until Nothing went out in the dark with only a small torch to light his way. When he came to the place where the trail had been greased he slipped, and he fell into the pit Anansi had dug and died on the sharpened wooden stakes. Anansi fled.

The people of the village grieved for Nothing. His servants and his wife and his friends mourned for him, for he had been a good man.

His wife cooked up many yams and made a sweet food out of them and carried it around to all the houses in the district. She gave some of the food to all the young children she met, and asked them to help her cry for her dead husband.

That is why so many children say, when you ask them what they are crying for,

"For Nothing."

HOW SOKO BROUGHT DEBT TO ASHANTI

ONCE a hunter named Soko came to the country of Ashanti from the town of Mina. Soko was not an Ashanti man, but he married a woman from Komasi and lived with the Ashanti people. Soon he talked the same language as the Ashanti and people began to forget that he was a stranger, except for one thing. Soko owed money. He had owed money before he came to Ashanti. People began to worry about it, because until Soko came no one in Ashanti had been in debt. Now there was debt in Ashanti, and people didn't like it. So some of the old men of his village went to him and said:

"Before you came there was no debt here. You must get rid of it."

Soko thought about the problem. It was true, he must get rid of his debt. He didn't know how to do it. But one morning when Soko was making wine from the juice of an oil palm, Anansi came along.

"Anansi, you are a clever fellow, how am I going to get rid of my debt?" Soko asked.

Anansi thought.

"That's very simple," he said. "Just say, 'Whoever drinks this palm wine takes the debt.' Then someone will drink the wine and he will have the debt."

"A fine idea," Soko said. "Whoever drinks this palm wine takes the debt."

"How about letting me have a drink of palm wine?" Anansi asked.

"Very well, help yourself," Soko said.

Anansi drank the palm wine, which was what he really wanted in the first place.

"Now you take the debt," Soko said. "I don't have the debt any more!"

So Anansi took the debt. He went back to his farm and planted some grain. "Whoever eats my grain takes the debt," Anansi said.

The grain grew up. Then one day a bird flew down from its nest in the forest and ate Anansi's grain. "Ha, now you take the debt!" Anansi said. "I don't have the debt any more!"

The bird flew back to her nest. She had the debt. But she laid some eggs in her nest and said, "Whoever breaks my eggs takes the debt." Then she flew off. And while she was away the wind blew and a branch broke off from the tree. It fell in the nest and broke the eggs. When the bird came back and saw what had happened she said to the tree, "Well, now you have the debt. I don't have the debt any more!"

The tree had the debt. But she grew some blossoms on her branches and said, "Whoever eats my blossoms takes the debt." A monkey came along and ate the blossoms in the tree, and the tree said, "Now you have the debt, I don't have the debt any more!"

The monkey had the debt. But he said, "Whoever eats me takes the debt." And a lion came along and caught the monkey and began to eat him. "Wah," the monkey said, "now you take the debt!"

The lion had the debt. He wandered around the forest with it. "Whoever eats me takes the debt," he said.

The Ashanti didn't have the debt any more, it was in the forest. But one day Soko came hunting in the forest and he killed the lion. He took the meat back to the village and shared it with the Ashanti. They ate it, and that is how debt came to stay with the Ashanti people.

HUNGRY SPIDER
AND THE TURTLE

SPIDER was a hungry one, he always wanted to eat. Everybody in Ashanti knew about his appetite. He was greedy, too, and always wanted more than his share of things. So people steered clear of Spider.

But one day a stranger came to Spider's habitation out in the back country. His name was Turtle. Turtle was a long way from his home. He had been walking all day in the hot sun, and he was tired and hungry. So Spider had to invite Turtle into his house and offer him something to eat. He hated to do it, but if he didn't extend hospitality to a tired traveler it would get around the countryside and people would soon be talking about Spider behind his back.

So he said to Turtle:

"There is water at the spring for you to wash your

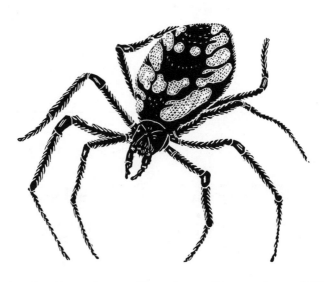

feet in. Follow the trail and you'll get there. I'll get
the dinner ready."

Turtle turned and waddled down to the spring with
a gourd bowl as fast as he could. He dipped some
water from the spring and carefully washed his feet
in it. Then he waddled back up the trail to the house.
But the trail was dusty. By the time Turtle got back
to the house his feet were covered with dirt again.

Spider had the food all set out. It was steaming,
and the smell of it made Turtle's mouth water. He
hadn't eaten since sunrise. Spider looked disapprov-
ingly at Turtle's feet.

"Your feet are awfully dirty," he said. "Don't you
think you ought to wash them before you start to
eat?"

Turtle looked at his feet. He was ashamed, they were so dirty. So he turned around and waddled as fast as he could down to the spring again. He dipped some water out of the spring with the gourd bowl and carefully washed himself. Then he scurried as fast as he could back to the house. But it takes a turtle a while to get anywhere. When he came into the house Spider was already eating.

"Excellent meal, isn't it?" Spider said. He looked at Turtle's feet with disapproval. "Hm, aren't you going to wash yourself?"

Turtle looked down at his feet. In his hurry to get back he had stirred up a lot of dust, and his feet were covered with it again.

"I washed them," he said. "I washed them twice. It's your dusty trail that does it."

"Oh," Spider said, "so you are abusing my house

109

now!" He took a big mouthful of food and chewed it up, looking very hurt.

"No," Turtle said, sniffing the food, "I was just explaining."

"Well, run along and wash up so we can get on with the eating," Spider said.

Turtle looked. The food was already half gone and Spider was eating as fast as he could. Turtle spun around and hurried down to the spring. He dipped up some water in the gourd bowl and splashed it over his feet. Then he scrambled back to the house. This time he didn't go on the trail, though, but on the grass and through the bushes. It took him a little longer, but he didn't get dust all over his feet. When he got to the house he found Spider licking his lips.

"Ah, what a fine meal we had!" Spider said.

Turtle looked in the dish. Everything was gone. Even the smell was gone. Turtle was very hungry. But he said nothing. He smiled.

"Yes, it was very good," he said. "You are certainly good to travelers in your village. If you are ever in my country you may be assured of a welcome."

"It's nothing," Spider said. "Nothing at all."

Turtle went away. He didn't tell other people about the affair at Spider's house. He was very quiet about his experience there.

But one day many months later Spider was a long distance from home and he found himself in Turtle's country. He found Turtle on the shore of the lake getting a sunbath.

"Ah, friend Spider, you are far from your village," Turtle said. "Will you have something to eat with me?"

"Yes, that is the way it is when a person is far from home—generosity merits generosity," Spider said hungrily.

"Wait here on the shore and I'll go below and prepare the food," Turtle said. He slipped into the water and went down to the bottom of the lake. When he got there he set out the food to eat. Then he came to the top of the water and said to Spider, who was sitting impatiently on the shore, "All right, everything is ready. Let's go down and eat." He put his head under water and swam down.

Spider was famished. He jumped into the water to follow Turtle. But Spider was very light. He floated. He splashed and splashed, kicked and kicked, but he stayed right there on top of the water. For a long time he tried to get down where Turtle was eating, but nothing happened.

After a while Turtle came up, licking his lips.

"What's the matter, aren't you hungry?" he said.

111

"The food is very good. Better hurry." And he went down again.

Spider made one more desperate try, but he just floated. Then he had an idea. He went back to the shore, picked up pebbles and put them in the pockets of his jacket. He put so many pebbles in his pockets that he became very heavy. He was so heavy he could hardly walk. Then he jumped into the water again, and this time he sank to the bottom, where Turtle was eating. The food was half gone. Spider was very hungry. He was just reaching for the food when Turtle said politely:

"Excuse me, my friend. In my country we never eat with our jackets on. Take off your jacket so that we can get down to business."

Turtle took a great mouthful of food and started chewing. In a few minutes there wouldn't be anything left. Spider was aching all over with hunger. Turtle took another mouthful. So Spider wriggled out of his coat and grabbed at the food. But without the pebbles he was so light again that he popped right up to the top of the water.

People always say that one good meal deserves another.

THROW MOUNTAINS

ONCE there was a boy named Toddu, who lived in the grass country north of Kumasi in Ashanti. He had to care for his father's cattle, and day after day he took them to the watering places and watched them graze. His father's herd had many cows and only one bull, but it was the largest bull in all Africa. Its name was Only One. Whenever a bull calf was born, Only One would kill it, for he thought one bull was enough for the herd.

One time a bull calf was born, and Toddu liked him very much. Only One didn't know about the calf yet, so Toddu carried him away into the bush country and hid him. Every day he crept back to the herd to get milk for the calf from its mother. The old bull, Only One, was getting suspicious about things, so when the calf was a little bigger Toddu took him far into the back country.

The calf grew up. When he was four years old he

was almost as big as Only One. Then Toddu took him to a great rock that lay in the middle of the plains and said, "You look like a bull, and you act like a bull. But you aren't full-grown until you're strong enough to move this rock."

The bull put his head down and pushed against the great rock, but nothing happened.

"You're too young, you're still a calf," Toddu said. "Wait another year."

The young bull was so provoked because he couldn't move the rock that he pawed the ground with his foot. He pawed so deep and wide that a lake came up, and that was Lake Bouro.

The next year the boy took his bull to the rock again and said, "Put your horns to it and try again."

The young bull put his head down and tried to toss the great rock, but it didn't budge.

"You're too young yet," Toddu said. "You're not grown up."

The bull was so angry he put one horn in the ground and charged through the bush, plowing a deep furrow. He plowed so deep and far that water came up and began to flow, and that was the Adifofu River.

They waited another year, and again Toddu said, "You're bigger now. Put your horns to the rock and push it."

114

The bull put his head down and pushed so hard his eyes got red and white foam came out on his hide, but the rock didn't move. He was so angry that he ran into the forest, tearing down all the trees for miles around. This was the great hurricane that Ashanti people still talk about.

Another year came, and the boy said to his bull,

"Try again." This time the bull dug his feet in and his muscles bulged and the rock swayed a little.

"Next year you'll do it," Toddu said.

But the bull was unhappy. He bellowed, and down in Komasi it sounded like thunder and the people ran for shelter.

The next year the bull was eight years old, and his horns were as thick as the trunk of a baobab tree.

"Try it again," Toddu said.

The bull tried the rock gently with his horns. Then he went a mile away across the flat grasslands. He pawed the ground, and then he began to run. He charged across the plains with his head down low, and struck the great rock in the middle. It smashed into many pieces and flew into the air in all directions. Wherever the pieces fell they became the mountains of Africa.

"Now you are ready," Toddu said. "Your name is Throw Mountains. Let us go find Only One."

They went out of the bush country to the place where his father's herd pastured. The cows were greatly surprised. Then Only One came.

"I am Only One," the old bull said. "Who are you?"

"I am Throw Mountains," the young bull said, "and you are not the only one any more."

Only One became angry and put his head down and pawed the ground. Then Throw Mountains put his head down and pawed the ground. They pawed so much earth they made a sandstorm that blew down to the coast and out to sea. They put their horns together and began to struggle. They trampled down a place a hundred miles wide where nothing will grow any more because they packed the earth so hard. Their breath came so hot that the palm trees wilted. They separated and then came together with such a crash that people thought cannons were shooting somewhere.

Only One spread his legs and tossed with his great horns, and Throw Mountains went flying into the air. He fell with a thump, and the place he landed became the deep hollow near Batooda. Throw Mountains got to his feet and shook himself. The two bulls rushed together again, and this time Throw Mountains threw Only One with a powerful toss of his thick neck. Twisting and turning, the old bull passed before the face of the setting sun, and the people in the east thought it was an eclipse. When Only One finally came to earth he fell in the northern mountains and flattened them, and it is through this flat country that traders make their way to Kumasi from Timbuctoo.

Throw Mountains became the chief of the herd,

and there was no more killing of bull calves when they were born.

Sometimes, before a storm, all the old cattle run and buck and jump like calves. This is because, like far-off thunder, they hear the distant bellowing of the great bull Only One.

ANSIGE KARAMBA, THE GLUTTON

ONCE in the village of Maku, in the country that lies between the Senegal and Gambia Rivers, there was a man by the name of Ansige Karamba.

Ansige was rich, for he had inherited much wealth from his father, but he was a miserly man and an incredible glutton. He had a wife named Paama and many servants and slaves. But he was a trial to them all. To Paama he was always complaining, "I never have enough to eat. You don't provide for me the way a wife ought to." Ansige was perpetually ill-mannered. He felt that the slaves and servants were eating too much, and robbing him besides. But they were really getting very little to eat, for Ansige hoarded his property so well that no one ever got anything out of him. The people of Maku thought that he

119

was the most impossible man they had ever known.

Ansige abused Paama with his complaints until she couldn't stand it any longer. So she went to him one day and said:

"I think I shall visit my father's village for a while. My family needs me." She took her things and left Maku for her home.

Now Ansige was more unhappy and more petulant than before. His meals were prepared by the servants, who cared for him less than his wife had. Whereas his food had been, in fact, rather good before she went away, now it was really bad, and there was less of it. The more he complained to the servants and slaves the worse things got, because they were quite tired of his greed and his gluttony.

One morning, after Paama had been away for a long while, Ansige said to himself:

"This is certainly a cruel situation. My wife ran away to her parents two years ago. Now I have to pay fabulous wages to ungrateful servants to prepare my meals, and they only cheat me and give me bad things to eat. I am practically dying of hunger. I shall get Paama and bring her home."

So he started out, and after a long journey he came to the village where his wife's parents lived. He went to their home, and there he was greeted by Paama's

father. As a gesture of hospitality Paama's father gave Ansige a young goat.

Ansige's mouth began to water. Forgetting everything else, he immediately took his goat out into a field, where he killed it and cooked it. He was very worried that someone might come along and want to share his meal with him. Even before it was quite done he began to gulp it down. He ate and ate. Before long the meat was all gone.

But Ansige was still hungry. He saw a large sheep grazing in the field. He caught it and killed it, and carried it to where his fire was burning.

He had been away from the village a long time, however, and Paama began to wonder where he was and what he was up to.

"I know my husband," she said to herself. "I had better go to see what kind of trouble his gluttony has gotten him into."

She went out to the field and found Ansige getting ready to cut the sheep up.

"What's this?" she said. "That isn't the goat my father gave you! It's a sheep that belongs to the chief!"

"Don't act as if you didn't know me," Ansige said petulantly. "I ate the goat your father gave me, but it wasn't enough. Then I saw this sheep, so I decided to round off my meal with him."

"Well, now you're in trouble," Paama said. "The chief will have you punished for killing his sheep. However, I'll get you out of it."

She made Ansige carry the dead sheep to where the chief's wild horse was tied, and they laid it down close by. Then they went back to the village. Paama stopped at the chief's house and reported to him that they had seen the sheep lying by the wild horse, and that the horse had kicked him and killed him. The chief sent a man out to see. "Yes," he told the chief when he returned, "the sheep must have been killed by the horse. It's an unfortunate accident."

The next day Paama said to her father, "If I know Ansige, he brought a great hunger along with him from Maku. What can I give him to eat that will satisfy him?"

"Why don't you give him some young roasted corn?" her father said. "That ought to quiet his hunger."

So Paama went out to the corn field and gathered a large basket of corn. There was enough corn for twenty men. She roasted it and took it to her husband.

Ansige ate it all. Not a single kernel was left. But his appetite was not stilled, it was simply aroused. He wanted more. So he went out to the fields. There he began breaking off ears of corn. When it was nearly dark Ansige picked up all that he could possibly carry and started off for the village.

He had trouble finding the trail, however, and it was getting darker and darker. At last he came out of the cornfield, but he couldn't see a thing, only the lights of the village. He started toward them, but between him and the village was a well. And when he came to the well Ansige fell into it with all his corn.

Meanwhile Paama, at home in her father's house, said to herself:

"I know my husband. I guess I had better see what he is doing. I wonder what kind of predicament his stomach has gotten him into now."

She went off to look for him, a torch in her hand. When she came to the well she heard him calling for help. She looked down with her torch, and there was Ansige, corn floating all around him.

"What are you doing down there?" she asked him.

"Don't act as though you didn't know me!" Ansige shouted. "I was just looking for something more to eat! People are trying to starve me to death! Get me out of here!"

"You certainly are in trouble! The people won't like it that you've been stealing their corn. But never mind, I'll help you out of this."

She went to where the cattle were, and chased them into the field where Ansige had been so busy. After the cows began to graze there Paama began to shout. People came running from the village.

"What is happening?" they said.

"A misfortune!" Paama said. "My husband was taking a walk when he saw the cattle in the field,

124

trampling the stalks and breaking off the ears of corn! He chased them and picked up the ears that had fallen off, but he is a stranger who doesn't know the trails, and he has fallen into the well!"

"Well, never mind," the people said. "It's not so bad. We'll get him up."

They chased the cows from the field and brought lights and ropes to pull Ansige out of the well. The first thing he did was to hurry back to the house for his dinner.

The next day Paama's father said to her:

"Today prepare something extra-nice for your husband to eat, something that he likes very much."

"I'll make millet dumplings," Paama said.

She put the millet in the wooden mortar and pounded it until it had become meal. Ansige looked on from a distance, hungrily. Four times she filled the mortar and made meal. There was a huge amount of it. She then mixed it with water and made the dumplings. When the dumplings were finished she brought them to Ansige. There were enough for twenty men.

But Ansige ate everything. And when the last speck of it was gone, he began to look longingly at the mortar in which the millet had been ground.

"Perhaps there is a little meal left in it!" Ansige said to himself. He went to the mortar and looked

down into it. Halfway down he saw some meal cling-
ing to the side. He put his head inside to lick the
meal off with his tongue. There was a little more in
the bottom. He pushed his head as far down as he
could. But when he tried to take his head out he
couldn't budge it. It was wedged fast.

Just about this time Paama was thinking:

"I know my husband. I ought to see what he is doing now. I'm sure his gluttony has gotten him into
some new kind of trouble."

She went to the house and looked around, but
Ansige wasn't there. Then she went out into the court,
and there she saw her husband head-down in the
mortar.

"What's going on?" Paama said.

"Don't stand there and ask me what's going on!"
Ansige said angrily from down in the mortar. His
voice sounded hollow and muffled. "I just stuck my
head in here to get a little more of the meal! Now I'm
wedged tight! Do something!"

"All right, all right," Paama said. "I'll get you
out."

She shouted for help, and the village people came
to see what was the matter.

"Ah, what bad luck!" Paama said. "And it's all
my fault! I told my husband he has a thick head, and

he said no, he doesn't have a thick head. I said his head was too thick to go in the mortar, and he said no it wasn't. Then he put his head in the mortar to show me and it got caught. It's all my fault!"

"Well, it's not so bad," the people said. They had to laugh, seeing Ansige bottom-side-up in the mortar. "But you must be right, he evidently does have a thick head!"

They sent for an ax, and with it they broke the mortar apart and got Ansige out. The whole village was amused. But Ansige was angry. He didn't like to have people laughing at him. He was so angry he took his things and went back to his village of Maku.

When he arrived there he remembered that he had been so busy eating that he had forgotten to tell Paama to come back with him. So he sent a servant to her to tell her to return at once. But Paama simply sent the following message to Ansige:

"Don't act as though I didn't know you."

DON'T SHAKE HANDS
WITH EVERYBODY

FROG had a large farm. When it was time to clear and plant he went to the village to get help, because it was more than he could handle alone. He asked the people of the village to come to clear his land, for the villagers always helped one another with their crops.

All the men of the village came. When they had cleared the land Frog fed them and thanked them for their help.

Then the great crowd of workers left his house. There were so many of them that they formed a line several miles long.

"I wonder what else I can do to express my appreciation for the goodness with which these people have treated me?" Frog said to himself. "I know, I'll shake hands with everyone who was here!"

He ran to the front of the long line of men and turned around to wait for them.

As the first man came to where he stood, Frog grabbed his hands enthusiastically and shouted:

"Oh, thank you! Thank you!"

He let go and grasped the hands of the second man, and shouted again:

"Oh, thank you! Thank you!"

He grabbed the hands of the third man and shouted:

"Thank you! Thank you!"

There were some strong men among the workers who, when they shook hands with Frog, squeezed very hard. There were so many of them that after a while Frog's hands became flattened out. After they had all gone, Frog's hands hurt him from so much shaking, so he went to God to make a complaint.

God listened to Frog. He looked at Frog's flattened hands. Finally, after Frog was all through telling about his complaint, God said:

"You were a little overenthusiastic. Hereafter, when you wish to thank a crowd, send a messenger to the village and he will announce your gratitude."

Frog went away. His hands were still flat.

Sometimes now, when he looks at them, he says:

"Don't shake hands with everybody."

NOTES ON THE STORIES

The Cow-tail Switch, based on a parable found by George Herzog in Liberia, is a type of story which has a special attraction for the West African audience, in that the audience itself participates in the working out of the solution. When this tale is told in its native setting, the decision as to which son should receive the prize is apt to be left open, and long arguments ensue despite the fact that the correct answer is likely to be known to all the listeners. Many puzzles and riddles known in Liberia call for similar choices, and the audiences, composed primarily of grown-ups, enter the discussions with great heat and conviction.

The ornamented cow-tail switch, about which the argument revolves in this story, is known in many parts of West Africa. It is carried by chiefs and dance leaders and is symbolic of vested authority.

Kaddo's Wall is based upon a story taken by Leo Frobenius from the Togo people (volume 6 of his "Atlantis, Volksmärchen und Volksdichtungen Afrikas," Jena, 1921).

It gives expression to the common African feeling that people, especially rich people, should be generous. There are many West African stories about misers and the ill fate that ultimately overtakes them. The Ganna people who figure in this tale are mentioned in various old legends, which recall the glory of the old kingdom. Its cultivated and generous king is contrasted here with the hard-headed and selfish backwoods man-of-importance, Kaddo.

Small cowry shells, mentioned in this story and in *The Cow-tail Switch*, are used widely in West Africa to ornament carvings, houses, and various kinds of useful objects. Inlaid designs made of cowry shells are found on the walls of houses belonging to important men and on walls of buildings with ritualistic importance.

The corn grown in Kaddo's village is not our maize, but a variety of millet or sorghum, commonly referred to as "Kaffir corn." Grindstones are used in some parts of West Africa instead of wooden mortars for pulverizing grain.

Talk is based on a story heard in Nigeria by Harold Courlander from an Ashanti from Ghana. Animals and objects often talk in African folk tales, but in this story and in *The Singing Tortoise* the phenomenon is treated as something unusual.

While there is great respect in native Africa for the dignity of a high office and for the ruler or chief, people are quite ready to criticize or poke fun at established authority. One of the most frequent—and safest—ways of doing so is in mimic dances, songs, and stories. In *Talk* the image of the imperturbable chief, comes in for some subtle irony.

Specially carved ornate West African stools are, like European thrones, the property of chiefs or kings. A chief would not consider himself ready to conduct business in proper fashion unless he was formally seated. An old, dignified man without exalted rank may have a boy carry his low stool after him wherever he goes.

The One You Don't See Coming is based on a parable recorded by George Herzog in Liberia (George Herzog and Charles G. Blooah, "Jabo Proverbs from Eastern Liberia," by permission of the Oxford University Press, Oxford, 1936, and of the International Institute of African Languages and Cultures, London).

Meat is highly regarded as a food in this section of Liberia, but there is not much to be had since the old forests have been pretty well cleared away in the coastal region and the land has been converted to farming purposes. The game, consequently, has retreated inland. When large game is found, the hunter may retain a generous portion of it for himself, but the rest of it is cut up and divided by the village butcher. This division of game figures in an important way in the story *How Soko Brought Debt to Ashanti.*

Kassa, the Strong One is based on a story taken by Leo Frobenius from the Mende tribe ("Atlantis," vol. 8, Jena, 1922). The Mende people have an especially imaginative body of tales, many of them based on exaggeration, mockery, sudden contrast, play, and sheer fantasy. The unexpected ending of this story is rather unusual in African literature.

Anansi's Fishing Expedition is based on a story recorded by R. S. Rattray in Ghana ("Akan-Ashanti Folk-Tales," by permission of the Clarendon Press, Oxford, 1931).

We meet here with Anansi, the trickster figure, hero of in-numerable West African tales. Usually he is clever but at times is shown up for the worse. In some Ashanti stories Anansi is portrayed as a human character, in others as a spider. In parts of West Africa the trickster takes the form of the Hare, ances-tor of our own Br'er Rabbit. Anansi survives in Jamaica and elsewhere in the New World, often under the name "Nancy." The tale of Anansi's fishing expedition is known in the West Indies, being associated in Haiti with "Bouqui," the hero of many local stories of African origin.

Younde Goes to Town is based on a story taken in Accra, Ghana, by W. H. Barker and C. Sinclair ("West African Folk-Tales," by permission of George G. Harrap and Com-pany, London, and the Sheldon Press, London, 1917).

As do many West African stories, it reflects a keen awareness of the difference between the experienced people of the sea coast who are in touch with the big world, and the simple farming people of the interior who preserve their old customs more faithfully and look upon the people of the coast with envious suspicion.

The Singing Tortoise is based on a story recorded in Accra, Ghana, by W. H. Barker and C. Sinclair ("West African Folk-Tales," by permission of George G. Harrap and Company, London, and the Sheldon Press, London, 1917).

The *sansa*, here played by the tortoise, is a typically African musical instrument, sometimes called "thumb-piano" in

English. Strips of metal or bamboo are mounted over two bridges on a small wooden box. The box is held in the hands and the strips are plucked with the thumbs. The sound is gentle, faint, and tinkling; the instrument is used mainly by men, who walk around with it and sing to its accompaniment for their own entertainment.

Concern over being ridiculed by neighboring villages is strong in Negro Africa where gossip travels fast. Many stories deal with the penalties of unguarded talk or of not keeping a secret. The contemplative tone of the tortoise's song is not rare in African folklore.

Time is based on a parable recorded by George Herzog in Eastern Liberia. The personification of Time is one of the many examples which show that "primitives" are by no means incapable of abstraction, as is sometimes maintained. African folklore in many respects gives a faithful picture of native culture, despite the changes which increasing contact with western civilization imposes.

Time's philosophical remarks with which he sends off the disappointed delegation are closely translated from the African idiom.

The Messenger to Maftam is based on a story taken by L. J. B. Bérenger-Féraud from the Soninke tribe of Northwest Africa ("Les Peuplades de la Senégambie," Ernest Leroux, Paris, 1879).

Tongue-twisters, playing on words and punning are found

more frequently in Negro Africa than elsewhere in the "primitive" world, although this story seems to bear traces of Mohammedan influence.

Guinea Fowl and Rabbit Get Justice is based on a story taken in Togo by A. W. Cardinall ("Tales Told in Togoland," by permission of the author Sir Alan Cardinall, of the Oxford University Press, Oxford, 1931, and of the International Institute of African Languages and Cultures, London).

As all Africans know, the head of the Guinea Fowl is bare on top, a detail which is very important in the story. While loads are customarily carried on the head, in actuality hair is rarely worn thin from this kind of work. This tale has a unique, ironic flavor. It comments on the vagaries of social justice. In the end one error cancels out another, however, and everything comes out all right.

Anansi and Nothing Go Hunting For Wives, based on a story collected in Accra, Ghana, by W. H. Barker and C. Sinclair ("West African Folk-Tales," by permission of George G. Harrap and Company, London, and the Sheldon Press, London, 1917), is one of the many African "that's why" tales. The play on the word "Nothing" reminds us of "Nobody," the name taken by Ulysses in his encounter with the one-eyed giant.

How Soko Brought Debt to Ashanti was heard by Harold Courlander in Nigeria from an Ashanti from Ghana.

This is one of the many "how it began" stories of West Africa. It demonstrates that Africans were interested in explaining the origin of social institutions and conditions as well as physical phenomena. In an indirect way the story lays the blame for the institution of debt upon Anansi, the trickster, who figured out a way to get the palm wine from Soko and thus precipitated a chain of circumstances which distributed the debt among the Ashanti people.

Hungry Spider and the Turtle is based on a story recorded by Harold Courlander from an Ashanti in Ghana.

Once more the tables are turned on the clever trickster, this time by the slow Turtle. The Spider's exploitation of his guest is carried out through appeal to cleanliness. Cleanliness of the body and of the home is carefully observed in Negro Africa. Africans bathe in hot water in the morning and again in the evening after they have returned home from their daily tasks.

Throw Mountains is based on a story heard by Harold Courlander from an Ashanti in Accra, Ghana.

This story, with its epic conception and exaggeration, represents a genuine type of African cosmological tales.

Ansige Karamba, the Glutton is based on a story taken by Leo Frobenius from the Karamba people of West Africa ("Atlantis," vol. 6, Jena, 1921).

While the African man feels superior to the woman, yet in many ways he acknowledges her superiority, as he does in the story of *Kassa, the Strong One*, and more realistically here, where the foolish glutton is saved from punishment by his clever wife.

Don't Shake Hands with Everybody is based on a parable recorded by George Herzog in Liberia (George Herzog and Charles G. Blooah, "Jabo Proverbs from Eastern Liberia," by permission of the Oxford University Press, Oxford, 1936, and of the International Institute of African Languages and Cultures, London).

The handshake was introduced in the old days into West Africa through contact with Europeans. In Liberia every tribe has its own style of shaking hands. However, between tribesmen it is felt to be a somewhat pompous gesture.

Parables and proverbs are appreciated in native Africa at least as much for the sake of apt and unexpected application as for their intrinsic worth and literary quality. Soon after the arrival of our expedition to Liberia we received a formal visit by a few old dignitaries, who were later joined by some casual, younger men. The latter arose after a while but their lingering leave-taking unmistakably signified an unspoken request for the customary polite gift of some tobacco. After their satisfied departure, one of the older men expressed the idea that etiquette had been carried perhaps a little too far and explained his advice by quoting the parable.

GLOSSARY AND PRONUNCIATION GUIDE

African languages contain sounds which have no exact equivalents in English. For that reason, the guide gives the African words in a spelling which comes nearest to their actual sounds. Usually, *a* is close to the vowel in "father," *e* to that in "day," *i* to that in "meet," but short, *o* to that in "go," *u* to that in "cool," but short. In the guide, *ah*, *ay*, *ee*, *o*, and *oo* were written for these vowels. The accent is usually on the first syllable.

Accra (Ahkrah, accent on the second syllable), an old town and trading center in Ghana, now grown into a modern city.

Adifofu (Ahdeefofoo), a river in Ghana.

Adiri (Ahdeeree), a river.

Akim (Ahkeem), a province of Ghana.

Ama (Ahmah), a man's name.

Anancy or *Anansi* (Ahnahnsee, accent on the second syllable), the Ashanti name for the Trickster; in many stories, for Spider.

Anene (Ahnaynay), an Ashanti man's name, meaning Crow.

Ansige Karamba (Ahnseegay Kahrahmbah), a man's name.

Ashanti (Ashantee, accent on the second syllable), a large tribe which at one time ruled the Ashanti kingdom, in what is now the Gold Coast Colony.

Bahene (Bahaynay), a man's name.

Biafu (Beeahfoo), a man's name.

Bouqui (Bookee), the name of Trickster in Haitian folktales.

Bouro (Booro), a lake in Ghana.

Cavally (Kahvahlee, accent on the second syllable), a large

141

river on the boundary of Liberia in the east and Ivory Coast.

Congo Li Ba Jelema (Kongo Lee Bah Jaylaymah), a Mende man's name.

Deeba (Deebah), a man's name.

Ga (Gah), a language spoken in Ghana.

Ganna (Gahnah), a legendary kingdom in West Africa.

Gunde (Goonday), a man's name.

Iri Ba Farra (Eeree Bah Fahrah), a man's name.

Kaddo (Kahdo), a man's name.

Kassa Kena Genanina (Kahsah Kaynah Gaynahneenah), a Mende man's name.

Komasi (Komahsee), or *Kumasi* (Koomahsee), a seacoast city in West Africa.

Kundi (Koondee), a village.

Maftam (Mahftahm), a town.

Maku (Mahcoo), a village.

Mamadi (Mahmahdee), a man's name, probably of Arabic origin.

Mende or *Malinke* (Menday, Mahleenkay), a large tribe whose territory stretches over large areas in Northwestern Africa.

Mina (Meenah), a town.

Minu (Meenoo), a man's name.

Ogaloussa (Ogahloosah), a man's name.

Ogo (Ogo), a man's name.

Osansa (Osahnsah), a man's name.

Paama (Pahmah, the first syllable long), a woman's name.

Puli (Poolee), a man's name, meaning "Hunter," in Liberia.

sansa (sahnsah), an African musical instrument.

Seno (Sayno), one of the old West African kingdoms.

Sogole (Sogolay), a man's name.

Soko (Soko), a man's name.

Soninke (Soneenkay, accent on the second syllable), a group of tribes in West Africa.

Tendella (Tayndaylah), a village.

Toddu (Toddoo), a man's name.

Younde (Yoonday), a man's name.